D0667577

"Between Heaven and Earth...

...is a bowlful of happiness!"

何鴻毅家族基金
THE ROBERT H. N. HO
FAMILY FOUNDATION

CnC
設計及文化研究工作室
DESIGN AND CULTURAL
STUDIES WORKSHOP

China
INSTITUTE

BOWLS *of* HAPPINESS

Treasures from China and the Forbidden City

Written by Brian Tse

Illustrations by Alice Mak

Translation by Ben Wang

WHEN MY FATHER, Robert H. N. Ho, decided to establish a family foundation to support Chinese culture and Buddhist philosophy, it was a modest beginning to facing a formidable challenge: how to preserve and make more accessible globally the treasure trove which is embodied in over 5,000 years of Chinese history and culture. Since 2005, The Robert H. N. Ho Family Foundation, based in Hong Kong, has been active around the world, supporting cultural projects and academic exchange in collaboration with museums, galleries, universities, artists, curators, and scholars. Education has been a common thread running through all of our foundation's work, especially the development of cultural awareness amongst the emerging generation of young Chinese who, not unlike their counterparts around the world, have been swept away by the compelling amusements of the Internet and 21st century youth culture.

Chinese parents, like parents around the world, are concerned that their children might lose their connection with their cultural roots. It was with that in mind that our foundation decided to support Mr. Chiu Kwong-chiu and his team at Design and Cultural Studies Workshop in Hong Kong, to develop a series of books, *We All Live in the Forbidden City*, using the theme of Beijing's ancient palace as a platform to educate young people about many important aspects of Chinese history and culture. The books and related outreach activities have proved to be a popular and engaging way to inform as well as "edutain."

Having supported these publications both in Hong Kong (published in traditional Chinese characters) and in mainland China (published in simplified Chinese characters), it is only natural that we make these award-winning books more widely available to an English language audience. As urban areas in North America, Europe, and the Antipodes become increasingly multi-cultural, so has our world become smaller with the increasing interdependence, economic and otherwise, between East and West. It is crucially important that young people learn more not just about their own culture, but also explore other cultures as well. My family and I hope this wonderful English language version, developed in collaboration with China Institute in America and Tuttle Publishing, will help bridge the gap between East and West, and continue to inform and entertain young people around the world.

Robert Yau Chung Ho
Chairman
The Robert H. N. Ho Family Foundation

THE ANCIENTS BELIEVED that the star of *Ziwei*, also known as Polaris, never changed its position. They believed that the star was enclosed by a purple bright constellation and that it was the home of the Great Imperial Ruler of Heaven. In China, the emperor was thought to be the son of the Great Imperial Ruler of Heaven, and this was how his palace came to be called the Purple Forbidden City.

In 1421 the third Ming dynasty emperor, Yongle, working with the collective power of the nation, finished construction on this majestic palace in Beijing. The Forbidden City occupies a total area of 720,000 square meters. Flanking its four sides are colossal city walls and a broad palace moat. Together these protect a sprawling landscape of towers, halls, and pavilions, made up of red bricks and golden roof tiles.

For almost 600 years, the Forbidden City was the home of the Chinese emperor. It contained a stupendous amount of masterpieces and rare treasures, which were handed down from generation to generation. Countless imperial and historical events occurred here through the vicissitudes of time. Eventually, the Chinese Revolution of 1911 overthrew the imperial system that had ruled China for thousands of years. Then, in October of 1925, the Palace Museum was established on the grounds of the existing palace. On that day, the Forbidden City opened its doors to the public and, ever since, the palace has taken on the role of a spiritual home and cultural heritage site for everyone to enjoy.

Today, the Palace Museum is the world's largest and most well preserved royal architectural complex. Around 1,800,000 pieces of historical artifacts are stored inside. Every year, it welcomes tens of millions of visitors, as its allure and splendor increasingly attract greater attention from around the globe.

The Hong Kong-based scholar Mr. Chiu Kwong-chiu is someone who has planted his roots in the Forbidden City. He and his team, the Design and Cultural Studies Workshop, research and interpret the subject matter deeply and earnestly. Mr. Chiu's passion for the Forbidden City is evident in all of his books, from *The Grand Forbidden City – The Imperial Axis to The Twelve Beauties* to this current series, *We All Live in the Forbidden City,* which has been designed for a younger audience. Especially in this series of illustrative books, Mr. Chiu's unique perspective, along with the dynamic use of language and drawings, enliven and animate the Forbidden City, a place that is austere and lofty in nature. Through these books, you will experience the palace's grandeur, but you will also find delight in its refined elegance. In a joyful manner, everything that is unique about the Forbidden City comes to life.

It made me very happy to learn that the English editions of several books from *We All Live in the Forbidden City* would be published in New York. By way of these books, I hope that the children in North America will find themselves being transported on a colorful journey to the Forbidden City, as they develop their understanding of Chinese history and culture.

I wish everyone an exciting voyage!

Shan Jixiang
Director
The Palace Museum

"Chirp"

"Chirp!"

HAPPINESS

Joyful Meetings

Mommy says, "At the sight of Piggy,
my heart leaps with joy!"
That's because my nickname is Piggy.

Mommy remembers when she picked me up,
right after I was born, with my pink body,
my wide cheeks, and my large nostrils.
"Oink, oink, oink!" I cried and cried, just like a piggy.
So Dad said, "Might as well call her Piggy!"

Whenever she sees a piggy, Mommy can't help breaking into a smile and saying, "*That* piggy reminds me of *my* darling Piggy!"

Mommy is good at making pottery.
She has made a bowl, and on the bowl
she painted a piggy.

Holding the bowl, Mommy smiles and says,
"At the sight of Piggy, my heart leaps with
joy!" Oh, silly Mommy!

Mommy says, "Now, should we add a few white clouds?"

The white clouds stretch their arms lazily into the big, big sky.

When Piggy sees them, she'll love them for sure!

"Seeing Piggy makes me happy too!" says White Cloud. "From up high, I love to watch pigs playing in the rich earth."

As they were talking, Mommy added a pair of butterflies onto the bowl. She says, "Between the vast sky and the big earth are beautiful butterflies." White Cloud and Piggy shout, "Seeing butterflies makes us happy too!"

Butterfly says, "Well, seeing Flower makes me happy!" Flower says, "I'm happiest when I see Butterfly!"

Piggy says, "I'm happiest when I see Butterfly and Flower together." White Cloud smiles in agreement.

"Don't forget about us! We're right between the sky and the flowers." Suddenly a pandemonium of parrots flies down from the sky, twittering and singing.

"I can sing, too!" Piggy says to the birds.

White Cloud says, "I'm coming down!"
and softly lands upon a lotus pond.

Now the goldfish in the water look like they
are flying in the sky. Tiny GoldFish gasps,
"What? There's a pig in the sky.
What a wonderful sight!"

Some bats have even come to join the party! White Cloud wonders, "Let's see who can move faster, the bats or Piggy!"

White Cloud then turns itself into drops of rain and showers down upon them. "Run! Let's run!" Piggy and the bats scream.

Mom says, "All this
playing must be tiring. How about some
fresh fruit for Piggy?" Piggy says, "Okay!"

Mommy paints some melons and other fruits onto
the bowl. She says these fruits represent the joyful
meeting of all living things.

The Whole World Celeb

Yes, this is the very bowl that Mommy has given me. Don't you think it's lovely?

Holding the bowl Mommy has given me, I look at Mommy; I look at the bowl. It makes me glad!

There are so many lovely things joined together on it, all gifts of happiness from Mommy to Piggy, which is me. Mommy smiles and says, "Oh, silly Piggy!"

"Chirp"

"Chirp!"

WHAT HAPPINESS!

A Mutual Blessing

WISHING FOR THE BEST

The sky and earth meet to create all living things. People meet these natural wonders to create happiness.

Yes, happiness can indeed be created! In Chinese culture, when babies are born, Mommies and Daddies name them based on the good things that have happened in their lives and the hopes that they have for their child's future. In these names they use sounds like *mei*, which means beautiful, or *wei*, which means powerful. (What does your name mean?) These babies are already creating happiness before they wear their first diaper!

Chinese people like to give auspicious names to lots of things. ("Auspicious" means to have good fortune.) For example, there is a street called the Boulevard of Eternal Peace in Beijing. There are dishes with names like Eight Treasure Rice. Even the name of Coca-Cola in Chinese can be translated as Tasty & Enjoyable (*kekou kele*).

"Chirp"

"Chirp!"

IN LIFE

Some names use images to convey meanings. A good example would be the Moon Cake, eaten at the Mid-Autumn Festival when the moon is most round. The round shape of the cake, and the full moon, symbolizes harmony, and a family being together for the holiday.

There are many words in Chinese with the same or similar sound. Therefore, it is possible to use these sounds to unite things that would otherwise have nothing to do with each other. For example, the pronunciation of 'cake' in Chinese happens to be the same as that for the word 'tall' (*gao*); 'sheep' sounds like 'auspicious' (*yang* and *xiang*). The word for 'bat' sounds the same as the word for 'happiness' (*fu*). That's why, in China, bats are symbols of happiness! Because different sounds in Chinese can sound like many happy things, blessings and good wishes can be heard from all directions, like the sound of chirping birds in the forest.

These blessings are something special in Chinese culture. It has led people to remark that the Chinese people love good wishes, while others have said this makes them too superstitious. To look at it another way, these are lovely feelings that can touch anyone. The greatest happiness lies not just in Heaven, or only on Earth, or with one person. It can be found in the relationships between nature and people, between people and things, and ultimately between people and people – just as happiness lies in the love between Piggy and Mommy.

Let's imagine you have a bowl just like the one Mommy made for Piggy. When you are eating from this bowl, a pretty painted flower will greet you. You will be happy. You will thank the flower, the bowl, and the person who made the tasty food. This is a moment when we have created happiness between us. Hopefully, children all over the world can experience the happiness of these Chinese blessings.

"Oink"

"Oink!"

These two bowls were not used for eating. Chinese emperors used them for important rituals that paid respect to Heaven and Earth. The blue color on this bowl symbolizes the sky; therefore it was used in rituals to honor Heaven.

The yellow color on this bowl symbolizes the earth and was used in rituals to honor Earth. Thank Heaven and thank Earth for giving us the four seasons and the natural wonders of the world!

"AREN'T THEY LOVELY?"

In the Palace Museum in Beijing, China, there is a great collection of porcelain bowls that were used by the emperors of China's last imperial dynasty, called the Qing. Piggy has seen many of the images painted on the bowls. Can you recognize them too?

Let's look at the beautiful decorations on these bowls and explore the meanings hidden in the designs.

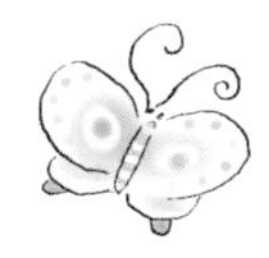

A YELLOW-GROUND FAMILLE ROSE 'BUTTERFLY' BOWL AND COVER

Butterflies are often seen on porcelain bowls because they often fly in pleasing pairs. The sound for butterfly in Chinese, *di-e*, sounds the same as the character that means 'to double.' So flying butterflies can symbolize double happiness entering a home. This bowl was made to celebrate the wedding of an emperor. When the empress saw it, she must have been very happy.

大雅齋

A YELLOW-GROUND GRISAILLE-DECORATED 'BUTTERFLY AND FLOWERS' BOWL

Here is that radiant yellow color again! The bright yellow gives the bowl a noble air, as this color could only be used for emperors and empresses. The blossoms and the butterflies look both dignified and graceful in the black and white style of Chinese ink paintings.

Here the butterfly meets the peony and hibiscus flowers. Peonies are called "the king of blossoms," and symbolize wealth and generosity. As for the hibiscus, the three Chinese characters in its name can sound like a phrase that means "wealth, glory, and prosperity." So the peony and hibiscus are saying, "While it's good to be wealthy, it's important to be graceful and elegant too!"

A GREEN-GROUND FAMILLE ROSE 'WISTERIA AND BIRD' BOWL

The green calls to mind the water of a clear lake, against which are set China roses and wisteria flowers. On a branch sits a singing laughingthrush bird.

As wisteria grows around and upon a tree and its branches, it evokes a sense of continuity and growth in life. The China rose blooms in all four seasons and is also called Eternal Spring Blossom. The singing bird and its song represent tenderness between loving couples. (Does your dad ever sing to your mom?) Judging from the excitement with which the bird is singing, might it be a lovable chirping mom?

大雅齋

A FAMILLE ROSE 'LOTUS AND EGRETS' BOWL

The background on this bowl is glazed in white with a thin gold border that threads around its rim. This gives the bowl a quiet elegance, with an air of wealth Lotus blossoms grow in muddy waters, yet always look lovely and clean, so they can represent an honorable person. In China, when the sounds for the words 'lotus blossom' and 'egret' are put together, they sound like the popular phrase, "May your journey be smooth and peaceful," the Chinese version of "Bon Voyage!"

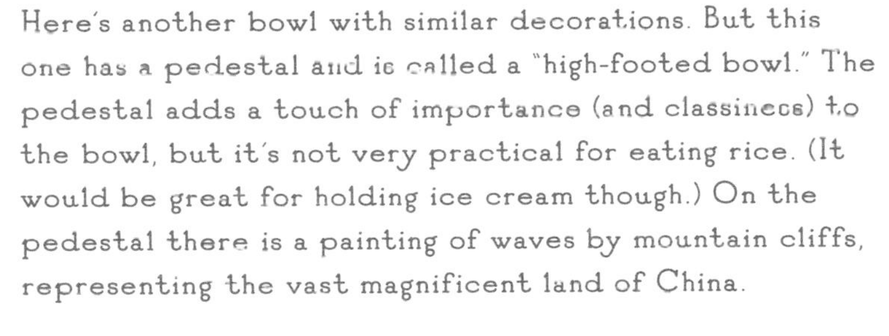

Here's another bowl with similar decorations. But this one has a pedestal and is called a "high-footed bowl." The pedestal adds a touch of importance (and classiness) to the bowl, but it's not very practical for eating rice. (It would be great for holding ice cream though.) On the pedestal there is a painting of waves by mountain cliffs, representing the vast magnificent land of China.

So, what flavor ice cream would you eat from this high-footed bowl? Chocolate? Green tea? Hmm...maybe mango sorbet?

(A high-footed bowl is usually used at ceremonies and rituals.)

A FAMILLE ROSE 'COILING VINE AND BITTER MELON' BOWL

The ripened seeds breaking out from the bitter melon on this bowl symbolize an abundance of children and grandchildren. Emerald green bamboo and morning glory flowers are also painted on the bowl. They coil from the outside of the bowl to the inside. So when someone finishes eating rice from this bowl, he or she will be surprised to see a butterfly inside. What a happy sight!

Because bamboo, hollow on the inside yet enduring as a tree, stands for modesty and honor, it joins with the vines and melons to represent not only an abundance of children, but also fine and talented children at that!

A YELLOW-GROUND FAMILLE ROSE 'FIVE BATS' BOWL

We already know that bats symbolize happiness. But did you know that peaches symbolize longevity? In China, sweet buns in the shape of peaches are often served at birthday parties to wish a happy birthday with many, many more to come.

Of the five types of happiness in Chinese culture, longevity is the most important, followed by wealth, good health, doing good deeds, and beautiful old age, in that order.

Here we see groups of bats representing all five kinds of happiness. Each group of bats circles around a stylized version of the character for longevity. Between each group of bats we see, tied with colorful ribbons, an ancient symbol for good luck. These combined images deliver a blessing of longevity, happiness, and good fortune.

These bowls show just a few examples of auspicious symbols used in Chinese art. They are just a small part of all the treasures found in Chinese culture...

"I am a gold fish. (I symbolize gold and jade!)"

"I am a small piggy. (I symbolize lots of food!)"

LET'S MAKE A BOWL

FLARING RIM

"Flaring Rim" indicates that the rim of the bowl curves out slightly.

RING FOOT

"Ring Foot" is the circular base on the bottom of the bowl.

CURVED WALL

"Curved Wall" refers to the graceful curvature on the body of the bowl.

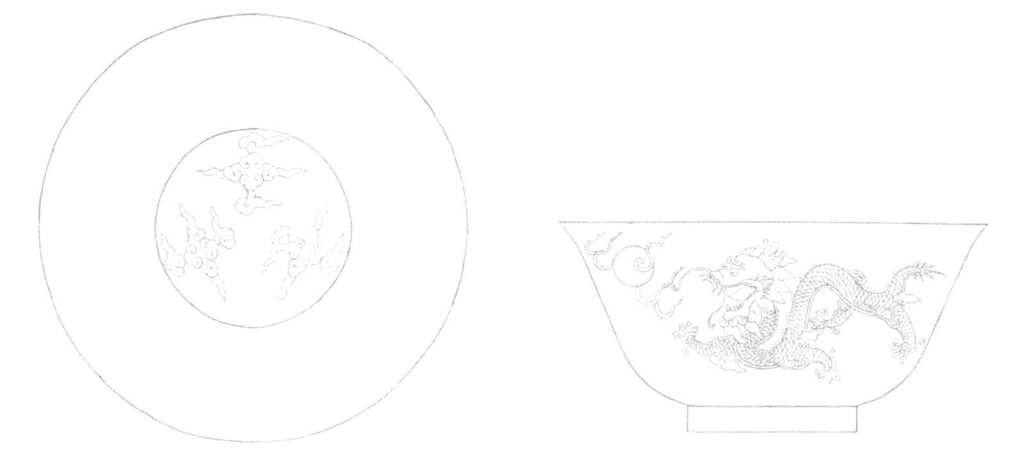

When a bowl is filled with hot soup, a "Flaring Rim" and "Ring Foot" will insulate against the heat so that the hands holding it do not get burned.

"Flaring Rim" and "Ring Foot" are Chinese designs that help fellow dinner guests serve food to one another. Together with long chopsticks these designs allow people to extend hospitality to fellow diners by serving one another. Eating together at the same table, everyone takes care of one another.

This pure white bowl looks simple and elegant, but it actually has decorations on it. On the outside there is a dragon. The dragon symbolizes the emperor, so this is a bowl for use by the emperor. On the inside of the bowl there are patterns of clouds. If there are clouds then there will be rain. The rain will moisten the earth. (And splash down on pigs!)

Before applying colors to a porcelain bowl (through glaze or a style called polychrome), there must first be a blueprint, which is a draft design drawn on paper. It is harder to draw on porcelain than on paper, but a finished porcelain bowl is so much more beautiful than the original paper draft!

DOCUMENTARY PICTORIAL VASE ILLUSTRATING SCENES FROM THE IMPERIAL KILNS

What? A vase suddenly appeared!

This is a very interesting vase. It shows an imperial kiln, where the entire process of porcelain production is documented, from the selection of materials, to the production of molds, as well as the application of glazes and polychrome, the firing process, and court officials approving and collecting the works.

The following is a speech by a fine porcelain vessel: "Hello! I am a piece of polychrome porcelain. I originated from a pile of earth, and now I am standing before you. I hope that you like me."

A palm that is slightly curled
meets a palm that is slightly curled.
The two palms touch gently.
A new bowl is born.

The two palms
receive a bowl of rice.
The two palms
hold a bowl of soup.
Feeling love and cared for,
feeling rich and fulfilled,
feeling that between Heaven and Earth,
is a bowl full of Happiness.

THE HAPPINESS OF BEING TOGETHER

MY BOWL OF HAPPINESS

Name:

Age:

Wish:

IT HAS ALWAYS BEEN MY BELIEF that culture should not be confined by geography. In the 1980s I studied in two different places in France. The first place was a lovely small town in southeastern France; almost all the people and events I encountered reminded me of the village in Hong Kong where I was born. The second place was Paris. While I was writing about the Forbidden City, quite oddly I found myself thinking about the Louvre. Similarly, when I was in Athens admiring the Parthenon, a shadow image of the Hall of Supreme Harmony appeared in my mind. Though each place is distinct from the other, I saw that they tell a common story about people everywhere. Bit by bit, these thoughts became the nutrients with which I teach the younger generation about Chinese culture in the classroom.

Culture should be seen beyond the realm of policy. It is about all of our struggles and the things that we cherish and accumulate. We gasp in admiration of our cultures' accomplishments. Of course, occasionally, life also gives us a reason to sigh, but it is because of these sighs that we learn to appreciate the wonders of life.

I would like to take this opportunity to express my greatest gratitude to the scholars of the Palace Museum in Beijing for their expert guidance, to China Institute in America for their hard work in implementing the English edition of the book, and especially to The Robert H. N. Ho Family Foundation for their continued support to arts and culture over the years. We also want to express our gratitude to Brian and Alice for helping us bring this story to children in such a lively and appealing manner.

Chiu Kwong-chiu
Winter 2013
Design and Cultural Studies Workshop

WE ALL LIVE IN THE FORBIDDEN CITY

Bowls of Happiness:
Treasures from China and the Forbidden City

Written by Brian Tse
Illustrations by Alice Mak
Translated by Ben Wang
Edited by Nancy S. Steinhardt

Original Book Design by Design and Cultural Studies Workshop Limited, Alice Mak & Luk Chi-cheong. Book Design for the English edition by Arthur Gorelik & Design and Cultural Studies Workshop Limited.

Managing Editors:
Michael Buening, Eva Wen, and Yuyang Li

Printed in Shenzhen, China by
Regent Publishing Services.

First edition, 2015
10 9 8 7 6 5 4 3 2 1

ISBN 978-0-9893776-4-5
Library of Congress Cataloguing-in-Publication Data is available under
LCCN 2015937327

Distributed by Tuttle Publishing
* 364 Innovation Drive,
North Clarendon,
VT 05759-9436

info@tuttlepublishing.com
www.tuttlepublishing.com

China Institute
* 100 Washington Street,
New York, NY 10006

www.chinainstitute.org
www.walfc.org

This book and all *We All Live In The Forbidden City*–related programming has been made possible through the generous support of the

何鴻毅家族基金
THE ROBERT H. N. HO
FAMILY FOUNDATION

www.rhfamilyfoundation.org

BOOKS IN THE *WE ALL LIVE IN THE FORBIDDEN CITY* SERIES

In the Forbidden City

This is the Greatest Place! The Forbidden City and the World of Small Animals

Bowls of Happiness: Treasures from China and the Forbidden City

What Was It Like, Mr. Emperor? Life in China's Forbidden City

---

ABOUT *WE ALL LIVE IN THE FORBIDDEN CITY*

In 2008 The Robert H. N. Ho Family Foundation collaborated with the Design and Cultural Studies Workshop (cnc.org.hk) in Hong Kong to create the *We All Live in the Forbidden City* (fc-edu.org) program. Using a contemporary voice and a variety of media formats, this program celebrates the Forbidden City and the study of architecture, imperial life, and Chinese cultural history in ways that are accessible, appealing, and relevant to children, parents, students, teachers, and the general public.

Working with China Institute in America, this program has now been brought to an English-language audience. Through four books, e-books, education programs, and a website, you will have the opportunity to learn about Chinese culture through this international icon. To learn more about the Forbidden City, WALFC, and to access games, activity guides, and videos, please visit www.walfc.org.

ABOUT CHINA INSTITUTE IN AMERICA

Since its founding in 1926, China Institute has been dedicated to advancing a deeper understanding of China through programs in education, culture, business, and art in the belief that cross-cultural understanding strengthens our global community.

SPECIAL THANKS

We at China Institute in America wish to express our gratitude to the many people who have worked with us on *Bowls of Happiness* and the *We All Live in the Forbidden City* program. Ted Lipman, Jean Miao, and Wong Mei-yee of The Robert H. N. Ho Family Foundation for their support and guidance in shepherding this project to North America. Chiu Kwong-chiu, Eileen Ng, Selina Wong, and Ma Kin-chung of the Design and Cultural Studies Workshop and Alice Mak, Brian Tse, and Luk Chi-cheong for creating such wonderful books and for their advice and collaboration in developing the English language editions. Wang Yamin of the Palace Museum, and the editorial team of Palace Museum Publishing House, for their vital support and expertise since this program's inception in 2008.

We also wish to thank: Qi Yue, Li Ji, and Yang Changqing at the Palace Museum; Christopher Johns at Tuttle Publishing; Samuel Ing, Adrienne Becker, Jacqueline Emerson, Olivia Cheng, Stephanie Ridge, Andrea Christian, Ben Wang, Nancy S. Steinhardt, and Arthur Gorelik.

Photographs courtesy of The Palace Museum Information Center and The Palace Museum Publishing House